JOURNEY TO THE GOLDEN LAND

By Richard Rosenblum

THE JEWISH PUBLICATION SOCIETY
Philadelphia–Jerusalem
5753–1992

Text and illustrations copyright © 1992 by Richard Rosenblum
First edition. All rights reserved.
Manufactured in the United States of America.
Book design by Edith T. Weinberg.
The Jewish Publication Society.
Philadelphia–Jerusalem.

LIBRARY OF CONGRESS CATALOGING-IN-PUBLICATION DATA
Rosenblum, Richard.
    Journey to the golden land/by Richard Rosenblum. — 1st ed.
      p. cm.
    Summary: Having left oppressive czarist Russia in search of better
living conditions, Benjamin and his family endure the difficult
journey and land at Ellis Island to start a new life in America.
    ISBN 0–8276–0405–x
    [1. Emmigration and immigration—Fiction. 2. Russian Americans—Fiction.]
    I. Title.
PZ7. R7191765Jo   1992
[E]—dc20   91–44941
                                              CIP
                                              AC

10 9 8 7 6 5 4 3 2 1

To my editors:
Alice Belgray, Anne Rosenblum, and Barbara Rosenblum

Benjamin lived with Mama, Papa, and his younger sister, Ruth, in a small village in a far corner of Europe that was part of Russia.

The Czar was the ruler of Russia, and his people feared him. He made cruel and unjust laws and used mean soldiers to enforce them. Many people could not choose where to live, where to go to school, or how to earn a living. Benjamin's family felt hopeless.

One day, Papa received a letter from his brother who had gone to America, the Golden Land. Papa's brother had worked hard to save the money that came in the envelope. He wrote that Papa and his family should come to America.

Benjamin listened to Mama's and Papa's discussions about what to do. They finally decided to make the long, hard trip and be free of the Czar, his unfair laws, and his soldiers. They would live a better life in America.

The family prepared to leave. They would only take what they could carry—clothes, photographs, Mama's feather quilt and feather pillows, and the brass holiday candlesticks that had once belonged to Great Grandmother.

The evening before they set off for America, the family said good-bye to all their relatives and friends in the village. Benjamin was scared about going so far away. He would miss his friends. He was sad because he might never see them again.

Papa hired a man with a wagon and horses to take them the many miles to the railroad station. They left their home in the middle of the night because they were afraid the Czar's soldiers might catch them. They did not have passports or documents and were traveling without official permission.

Everyone was grim and quiet. The children were scared. After two days and two nights, the wagon crossed the Russian border and entered a different country. They were no longer in the Czar's land. The family hugged and cried with relief. Now no one could send them back to their poor village or to jail.

A day later they came to the railroad station. They found many other travelers waiting.

The train arrived. Benjamin had never seen one before. The big locomotive thundered into the station, hissing and puffing. It was pulling many wooden cars.

Papa chose a car, and they climbed aboard. People carried on bundles, baskets, and even cages of chickens and ducks. Benjamin's family found a little space.

They ate the food they had brought from home and slept on the train. Once, they changed trains. After many days they arrived in the big city from where the boat would leave for America.

The family found their way to a hostel. Many more people like them were staying there to wait for the ship.

Papa and Benjamin went to the steamship company office and bought tickets with most of their precious money. They would sail to America on a ship called *The Amerika*.

They bought food for the trip, and, with a leftover coin, Papa bought Benjamin an orange from a woman on the street. Benjamin had never seen or eaten an orange before. He took it back to the hostel and shared it with Ruth.

At last it was time to go. Benjamin saw the steamship for the
first time. It sat in the water alongside the crowded dock. Passengers
called to each other, workmen and officials shouted, engines
chugged, men moved cargo, and the ship's horn boomed.

All the poor families were herded into steerage, an iron room deep down in the ship. They lived there during the fourteen-day voyage to America. The room was dark and smelled awful. There was a table in the middle where Benjamin's family ate the black bread, dried fruit, and salty herring that they had brought with them. The rumbling of the nearby engines and the rolling and rocking of the ship made many people sick.

The passengers felt happier when the weather was good, and they could sit outside on the deck, wrapped in shawls and coats to keep warm. Benjamin and Ruth played with the other children.

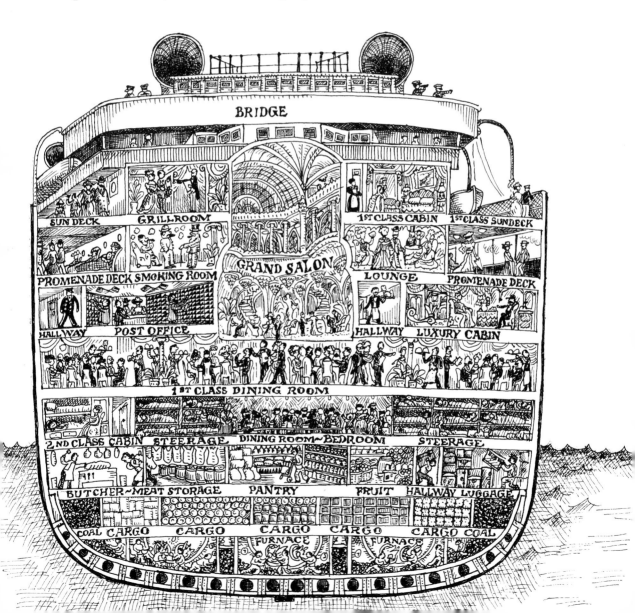

Finally, the ship reached New York. Along with most of the other passengers, Papa, Mama, Benjamin, and Ruth watched as they passed the Statue of Liberty. The statue had a very special meaning for them. They had arrived in America, a land where people could be free and lead better lives.

When the ship docked, the only passengers forced to remain on the ship were those in steerage class. Tags, telling who they were and where they came from, were pinned to their coats. Then they were put on a ferry and taken to a place called Ellis Island.

Papa and Mama had heard about Ellis Island. The people at the hostel and in steerage had talked about it. It was the last stop before they could be admitted through the Golden Door. Here they would have health examinations, and officials would question them.

Benjamin's family and all the others on the ferry who had come to make a new home in America were called immigrants.

When the ferry landed at Ellis Island, the immigrants were met by officials who spoke their languages. They led the crowd into the large building in front of them.

Inside, they heard many different languages spoken. The officials shouted at them and shoved them to the baggage room where they left their packages, bundles, bags, and baskets.

Benjamin held his father's hand, and Mama carried Ruth as they went up a long, steep stairway. Officials watched them as they climbed. They were searching for the lame and the weak. The officials would send these unfortunate people back to Europe.

At the top of the stairs was a very large, very noisy room, the
Great Hall.

Officials there pushed the immigrants into lines between iron rails. Benjamin stayed close to Papa until their turn came. A medical officer looked at their skin and hair and listened to their hearts. He sent them to another long line where another doctor checked their eyes for diseases.

A few people did not pass the examination. The doctors drew a chalk code on their clothes. Papa whispered to Benjamin that those people would have to go back on the steamship or stay on Ellis Island until they got better. Papa was glad that his family passed the physical part of the examinations. They were healthy enough to enter this new country.

Next, they sat on benches, terrified of the questions that the registration officer might ask. If Papa's answers were wrong, Benjamin's family could be sent back to Russia. Papa rehearsed his answers over and over.

Benjamin looked across the busy room at the big arched windows. He could see over the water to the city where his family hoped to live. Benjamin was worried about this final test, and he wondered if their turn would ever come.

Finally, an official summoned the family. An interpreter spoke for the official in their language. He asked their name. Papa said it was "Ptechfsky." He asked Papa to spell it. Papa couldn't. The official said their name would be "Rosenblum" like the family just before them. He knew how to spell "Rosenblum."

He asked Papa more questions. What was his occupation? How would he earn his living? Papa said he was a tailor. Had Papa ever been in prison? Finally, after many other questions, the man handed Papa a card that said ADMITTED. For the first time that day, they all smiled.

Now people were getting onto lines to exchange their foreign money for dollars. Papa said they had no money left to exchange.

Papa, Mama, Benjamin, and Ruth found their bundles and baskets and walked to a door that said PUSH TO NEW YORK. Benjamin was the first to walk through the door and into a room filled with waiting relatives. People embraced each other. Others were crying with happiness.

Benjamin's uncle was there, waiting. Papa hardly recognized his brother. He hugged and kissed Papa and Mama, and he gave candy to Benjamin and Ruth. They all went out onto the dock to wait for a ferry. It would take them across the harbor to New York, the city Benjamin had seen through the windows. Benjamin stood on tiptoe. He wanted a better view of his new city. At last the long journey was over. They had escaped.

Benjamin's family had arrived in the Golden Land and was about to start a new life with a new name.